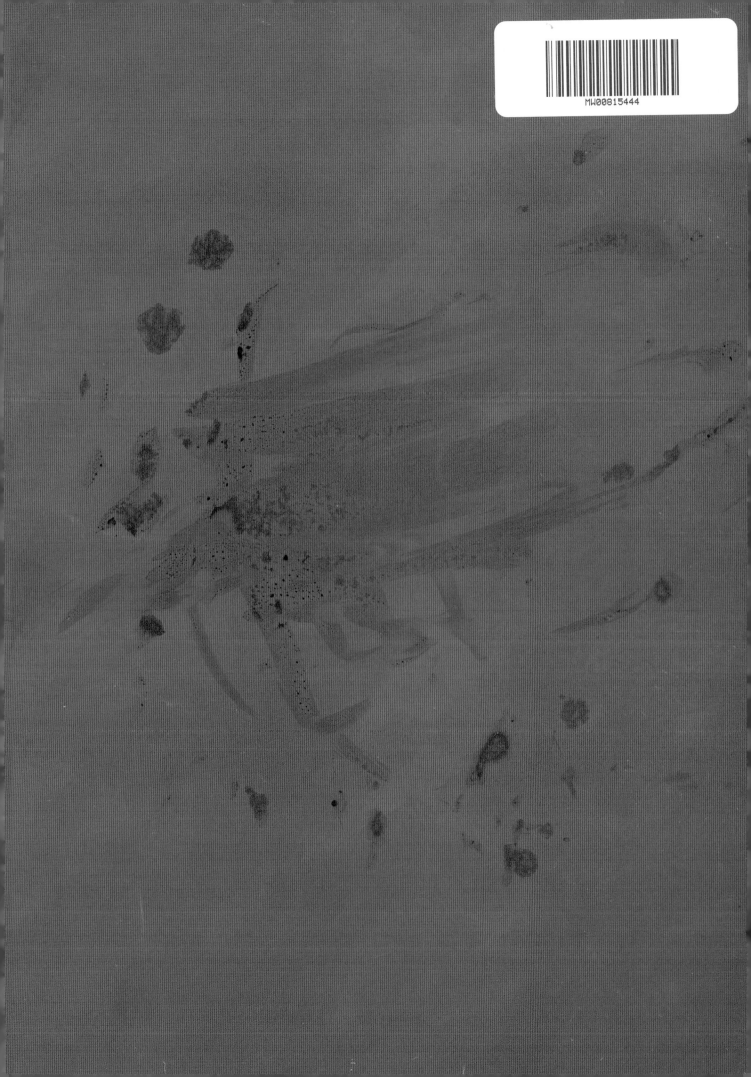

NorthParadePublishing

©2013 North Parade Publishing Ltd.
4 North Parade,
Bath BA11LF. UK
Printed in China.
www.nppbooks.co.uk

A Treasury of Christmas Stories

SCROOGE & MARLEY

A Christmas Carol

Once upon a time, on a Christmas Eve, Ebenezer Scrooge sat busy in his counting house.

A faded sign hung above his office door that read "Scrooge and Marley". Jacob Marley had been Scrooge's business partner, but he had died over seven years ago, and Scrooge was such an old skinflint he wouldn't even pay for a new sign to be put up.

It was cold, bleak, biting weather that day and the thick fog outside came pouring in through every chink and keyhole, but Scrooge never felt the winter chill, for he was a mean, tight-fisted old miser with a heart as cold as ice. He never did a kind deed or helped anyone, although he had piles of money locked away... and most of all he HATED Christmas!

All day long Scrooge left his office door wide open to keep his eye on his clerk, Bob Cratchit, even on Christmas Eve. The poor fellow was so cold he had to work in his coat and scarf. And the fire Scrooge allowed him to have was so small it looked like just one coal was lit.

"A Merry Christmas, Uncle!" cried a cheerful voice. It was Scrooge's nephew, Fred, who had called to wish him the very best for the festive season.

"Bah!" cried Scrooge. "Humbug!"

"Don't be angry, Uncle. Come and share Christmas dinner with us tomorrow," said his nephew, kindly.

The very word 'CHRISTMAS' made Scrooge angry. "If I had my way," shouted Scrooge, "every idiot who goes around wishing people 'Merry Christmas', should be boiled with his own Christmas pudding and buried with a stake of holly through his heart. Keep Christmas in your own way and let me keep it in mine!" And Scrooge pointed to be the door.

As he left, Fred stopped to wish Bob Cratchit a 'Merry Christmas'. The poor man was trying to warm his freezing hands by a candle flame.

The afternoon got foggier and darker and colder. A little boy bent down to sing a carol at Scrooge's keyhole, but at the first few notes of:

"God rest you, merry gentlemen,
May nothing you dismay..."

Scrooge grabbed his ruler and the poor boy fled in terror.

At last, the time came to stop work and close the office. Bob Cratchit blew out his candle and put on his hat.

"I suppose you want all day off tomorrow?" snapped Scrooge.

"If that's alright, sir," said Bob Cratchit timidly. "It's only once a year, and it is Christmas Day!"

"It is not alright," replied Scrooge. "Just remember that I will have to pay you a whole day's wage for no work!" and Scrooge left with a growl.

Bob Cratchit locked up the office in a twinkling. On the way home, just because it was Christmas, he went down an icy slide twenty times, just for the fun of it!

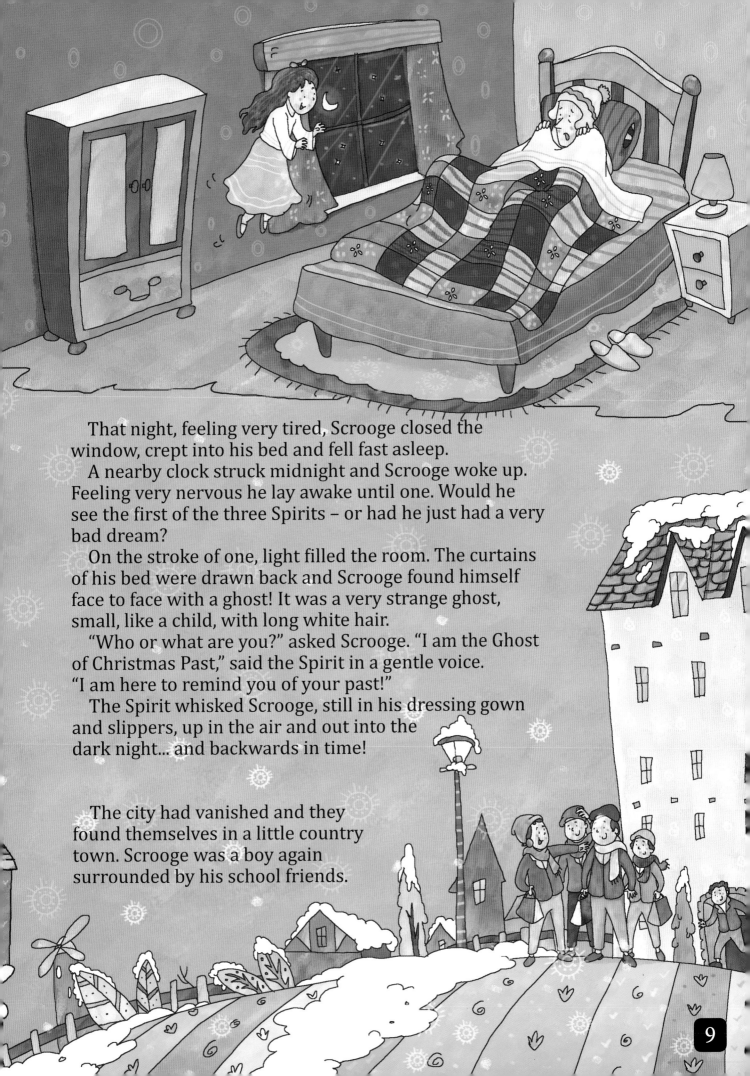

That night, feeling very tired, Scrooge closed the window, crept into his bed and fell fast asleep.

A nearby clock struck midnight and Scrooge woke up. Feeling very nervous he lay awake until one. Would he see the first of the three Spirits – or had he just had a very bad dream?

On the stroke of one, light filled the room. The curtains of his bed were drawn back and Scrooge found himself face to face with a ghost! It was a very strange ghost, small, like a child, with long white hair.

"Who or what are you?" asked Scrooge. "I am the Ghost of Christmas Past," said the Spirit in a gentle voice. "I am here to remind you of your past!"

The Spirit whisked Scrooge, still in his dressing gown and slippers, up in the air and out into the dark night... and backwards in time!

The city had vanished and they found themselves in a little country town. Scrooge was a boy again surrounded by his school friends.

9

All the boys were going home for the Christmas holidays. However, no-one came to fetch young Ebenezer that year. So he was left alone at school to spend a miserable Christmas all by himself.

When Scrooge remembered this he began to cry. The Spirit smiled and waved his hand. "Let us see another Christmas!"

Scrooge saw himself sitting in the schoolroom a few years later. Again all his friends had gone home for the Christmas Holiday.

Suddenly, the door opened and his beloved sister, Fran, darted in. She flung her arms round his neck and kissed him.

"I have come to bring you home, not just for the holidays, but for ever and ever!"

Quick as a flash, the Spirit whisked Scrooge away from his old school. In no time at all they were outside a warehouse door and the Spirit asked Scrooge if he knew this place.

"Know it? I was an apprentice here!" cried Scrooge excitedly.

They went in. Scrooge could see himself as a young gentleman, having a marvellous time at the office Christmas party.

His old boss, Mr Fezziwig, had ordered all his young apprentices to stop work and join the family in fun and games. There was music and dancing and presents for all.

Poor Scrooge remembered how happy he had been in those days, but now he cared more about money than friends. And he had forgotten how to dance and have fun.

The Spirit of Christmas Past had made Scrooge see what a lonely miserable old man he had become. Suddenly, Scrooge realised that he was back in his own bedroom. Tired out, he fell fast asleep.

All too soon he was woken in the middle of a huge snore by the clock striking one again.

As he peered over the bedspread, Scrooge saw the whole place filled with rosy light from the next room.

Trembling, he got up and shuffled in his slippers over to the door.

"Come in! Come in!" boomed a voice. "I am the Spirit of Christmas Present. Come in and get to know me."

Scrooge entered timidly, and what a sight met his eyes. The room was full to bursting with Christmas fare. And right in the middle sat a cheery fat giant of ghost.

"Touch my robe," said the Spirit of Christmas Present.

Scrooge did as he was told and held on tight.

Everything in the room vanished and Scrooge found himself walking through the cold snowy city streets, together with the Spirit.

It was Christmas morning and the shops were still open. The grocer's, the baker's, the poulterer's and the fruit shops, all selling Christmas food up to the very last minute.

Church bells rang out all over the city, calling folks to church. The streets were full of happy bustling people. Some were going to worship, while others were carrying their Christmas goose to the baker's, to be cooked in his huge oven. Everyone was looking forward to their Christmas dinner.

Quickly, the Spirit moved on with Scrooge still hanging tight onto his robe. At last they stopped and slipped, quite unseen, into the home of Scrooge's clerk, Bob Cratchit.

Now this poor fellow had to bring up his family on just fifteen shillings a week, for that was all that mean old Scrooge would pay him.

But today it was Christmas Day, and Mrs Cratchit had managed to save enough to make a Christmas dinner - a special dinner that all the Cratchits would remember until next Christmas.

As Scrooge and the Spirit gazed at the happy scene, Mrs Cratchit was busy laying the table for dinner, helped by her daughters, while a couple of the younger Cratchits danced around the room getting very excited.

Young Peter was in charge of a large pan of potatoes, bubbling away on the fire. Everybody was simply longing for dinner to be ready.

"Here's Father coming home," cried the two little Cratchits, as Bob came home from church with his youngest son, Tiny Tim, on his shoulders.

Young Tiny Tim was very frail. He had to use a little crutch, and could only walk with an iron frame strapped onto his leg. When he was tired he sat by the fire on his own small stool.

In rushed the young Cratchits carrying the small goose that had been roasting in the baker's oven. It was dinner time at least!

The dishes were put on the table and grace was said. Everyone took a deep breath as Mrs Cratchit plunged her carving knife into the hot roast goose, stuffed with sage and onion and served with apple sauce and mashed potatoes. It was just enough for the whole family.

Later, excitement grew as Mrs Cratchit left the room.

She returned, quite flushed, with a Christmas pudding - and what a pudding! It was speckled like a cannonball, blazing with brandy and a sprig of holly on top.

At last dinner was finished, and the whole family sat round the fire with roast chestnuts and some punch. Bob raised his glass. "A Merry Christmas to us all dears. God bless us!"

"God bless everyone!" said Tiny Tim, and Bob reached out and held his frail little hand.

"Spirit," said Scrooge, "tell me if Tiny Tim will live."

"I see an empty chair," replied the Spirit, "and a crutch without an owner. If things do not change, Tiny Tim will die!"

"No, no," said Scrooge. "Kind Spirit, say he will not die!"

Scrooge hung his head as he remembered how little money he paid Bob Cratchit. It was because of him Bob's family were so poor, so shabby and so often cold and hungry.

That night the Spirit of Christmas Present showed Scrooge many things. They visited places that made Scrooge shudder. They flew over bleak dark moors where miners worked underground. They flew over the raging sea and heard sailors singing carols as they steered the ship through a storm.

Worst of all they saw ragged hungry children with no-one to care for them, even at Christmas. It was then Scrooge remembered that he had never tried to help them, although he had been given many chances.

It had seemed such a long night and the Spirit and Scrooge had travelled far. A bell struck twelve again and the Spirit vanished.

As Scrooge looked again, he saw a dark figure drifting towards him through the mist.

"Are you the Spirit of the Future?" whispered Scrooge.

The Spirit did not answer, just pointed. He showed Scrooge people talking about a certain old miser who had just died. No-one was sad, no-one went to his funeral, no-one missed him or loved him.

Then, without a word, the Spirit of the Future took Scrooge to the home of Bob Cratchit. There he saw the sad faces of the young Cratchits, the empty stool by the fireside and the crutch in the corner. Scrooge realised that Tiny Tim must have died.

"Tell me about my future, Spirit!" begged Scrooge trembling, but the Spirit didn't reply. Instead he led him to a churchyard and pointed at a gravestone.

Scrooge crept towards it and written on the stone was his own name: EBENEZER SCROOGE.

EBENEGER SCROOGE

"That can't be me!" cried Scrooge. "I will change! I promise to keep Christmas in my heart all the year round!"

As poor frightened Scrooge tried to grab the Spirit's arm, the black robe collapsed and changed into a bedpost.

Yes, the bedpost was his own, the bed was his own and the room was his own. Best off all, he was alive with time in front of him to change his ways.

17

Scrooge jumped out of bed laughing and crying in the same breath. He rushed round the room dancing and singing, so happy that he put on all his clothes inside out and back to front.

Running to the window, he opened it and stuck his head out. "What day is it today?" he called to a boy dressed in his best clothes.

"Why, Christmas Day!" replied the lad.

"So, I haven't missed it," said Scrooge to himself.

Then he told the young boy to run and buy the huge turkey hanging in the poulterer's shop, and he gave the boy a half crown for his trouble.

"I'll send it to Bob Cratchit!" chuckled Scrooge. "He'll never guess where it came from. It must be twice as big as Tiny Tim!"

Having paid for the turkey and a man with a cab to take it over to Camden Town, Scrooge felt quite breathless.

No time to waste. Scrooge shaved, then dressed himself up in his best clothes. He went out into the street calling, "Merry Christmas," to passers by and smiling at everyone he met.

He went to the church and then walked towards his nephew Fred's house. He passed the door a dozen times before he plucked up courage to knock.

A girl let him in and Scrooge went straight to the dining room and poked his head around the door.

"Why bless my soul" cried his nephew, "who's that?"

"It's your Uncle Scrooge. I have come to dinner. Will you let me in?"

The family gave Scrooge such a warm welcome that he felt at home in minutes. He enjoyed a wonderful party with wonderful games – the old man never felt happier.

Next morning, Scrooge wanted to be first at the office (just to catch Bob Cratchit coming in late).

The clock struck nine, no Bob. Scrooge sat with his door wide open. At last at eighteen and a half minutes past nine, Bob arrived.

His hat and scarf were off before he opened the door. He jumped up on his stool and began writing away as fast as he could.

"What do you mean by coming here at this time of the day?" growled Scrooge, pretending to be angry.

"It's only once a year," pleaded poor Bob. "I promise it won't happen again!"

"I'm not going to stand this kind of thing any longer!" Scrooge went on, digging Bob Cratchit in the ribs. "And therefore I am about the raise your salary!"

Bob jumped back.

"A Merry Christmas, Bob," said Scrooge slapping him on the back. "A merrier Christmas than I've given for many a year. Build up the fire and we'll sit together and talk about your family."

Scrooge was better than his word. He did much more than he promised; and to Tiny Tim, who did not die, he was a second father.

Some people laughed at such a change in Scrooge, but he didn't care a bit.

He had no more visits from ghosts or spirits. And it was always said of him that he knew how to keep Christmas as well as any man alive.

May that be said of all of us. As Tiny Tim said - "God Bless Us, Everyone!"

The Little Fir Tree

Once upon a time, in a clearing deep in the middle of a great forest, there grew a Little Fir Tree.

All around him were giant pine trees with long straight trunks, their top branches almost reaching the sky – well at least, that's how it looked to the little Fir Tree, who longed to grow tall and tower over the whole forest.

The animals who lived nearby loved the Little Fir Tree. In spring and summer they played all day beneath his soft feathery branches. Small birds built their nests amongst his sweet smelling needles, sheltered from the strong winds that swept through the giant pines high above.

All day long, the Little Fir Tree could hear the second of axes ringing through the forest, as the woodcutters felled the tallest trees and brought them crashing to the ground.

The Little Fir Tree sighed to himself, "I wish my trunk was tall and straight enough to be ship's mast, or even the strongest beam in a big house."

With that, he stretched his small branches as hard as he could, to try and make himself grow a bit bigger.

One day, the wind that swayed the Little Fir Tree's branches began to grow colder and the first few snowflakes of winter started to fall.

The animals all disappeared for their long winter sleep, and most of the birds had flown away to warm summer lands. Very soon, the snow lay thick on the ground and even the woodcutters had left the forest until the next spring.

Was the Little Fir Tree lonely? No, because soon new exciting sounds began to fill the air. It was laughter and shrieks from happy children, as they tobogganed down the forest's snowy slopes.

Suddenly the Little Fir Tree felt some children tugging at his branches and then sawing his trunk. His was placed on sled and carried off down the slope as well.

At last they came to the small town at the foot of the forest's slopes. As the children ran through the streets, they shouted to everybody they met, "Look at our tree! Isn't it the most perfect Christmas Tree you ever saw?"

The little Fir Tree felt rather puzzled. "What on earth is a Christmas Tree?" he thought to himself.

The Little Fir Tree was beginning to enjoy himself. "This is much better than becoming one of those giant pine trees and living all your life in the forest," he thought.

"Where did you get that lovely little tree?" "Is he for sale?" "Please can I buy him?" people shouted as they passed by. The three children just grinned and shook their heads.

All that moment, the Little Fir Tree looked around. He saw fir trees everywhere! They were standing in windows, outside front doors, on porches and in gardens.

"These must be Christmas Trees," smiled the little Fir Tree, feeling proud. "Then I shall be the very best Christmas tree of all!"

When the Little Fir Tree reached the children's house, he was carefully carried inside and placed upright in a tub.

That night, the whole family gathered around to decorate their Christmas Tree, as it was Christmas time.

Everyone helped to hang the decorations on the Little Fir Tree's branches.
Soon this very special little tree was covered with toys and fruits, cookies
and candy, and lots of tiny candles. And at the very top – a golden star!

There stood the Little Fir Tree quivering with pride. He really was the most beautiful Christmas tree in the world!

The tiny candles twinkled like a thousand stars and filled the room with their sparkling light. The Little Fir Tree shone in all its glory, for it was Christmas Eve – the most magical night of the year.

Before they went to bed on this very special night, the children left their stockings beneath the Little Fir Tree. "No one has ever seen Father Christmas," whispered the children, very excited, "and he won't come until everyone is fast asleep."

And late that night father Christmas did come. He slipped silently into the room, quietly took the children's presents from his sack and popped them underneath the tree.

Just for the moment he stepped back to admire the beautiful Little Fir Tree. With a twinkle in his eye, he gave a broad smile, then vanished up the chimney.

The Little Fir Tree felt so happy to be a Christmas tree, and very Proud that he alone had seen Father Christmas.

During the twelve days of Christmas, the Little Fir Tree had a wonderful time. Many visitors called at the house to admire him, and lots of children came in from the street to see how beautiful he looked. The Little Fir Tree loved every moment of it, and thought it would last for ever.

All too soon the twelfth night came, which marked the end of Christmas. Every single decoration in the house was taken down and packed away until the following year.

The Little Fir Tree looked so bare. His needles had all dropped onto the floor and his branches were brittle and dry, but worse was still to come! Along with all of the other greenery left over in the house, the poor Little Fir Tree was taken outside and thrown onto the bonfire.

And that was the end of the Little Fir Tree! The whole family felt sad that Christmas was over and their lovely tree had met such a sad end. So, right there and then, the children's father made a promise that it would not happen again.

During the long cold months of winter that followed, the family never forgot their Little Fir Tree. The children remembered his dazzling brilliance, and it made them feel happy through the dark winter nights. Spring came at last. The warm sun melted the snow and ice and the forest came to life once more.

One bright sunny morning, Father took the three children to the spot where he had cut down their Little Fir Tree.

This time he took with him a spade and not an axe. Together they carefully dug up three trees – one for each of the children - a tiny tree, a medium sized tree and one a bit bigger.

Back home they planted the biggest tree in the garden, the medium size one near the house, and the tiny tree in a pot near the door.

So the next Christmas came they would have fir trees that would keep growing, and not have to be thrown out and burnt like their poor Little Fir Tree!

As years went by, the children decorated their trees every Christmas. On the two outside, they tied hundreds of glistening lamps. The smallest tree was carried inside every year until it grew too big for the house.

Now the children have grown up and have children of their own and grandchildren. The three fir trees have grown, and now they are the tallest in the valley. And every Christmas Eve, they shine so brightly, for all the world to see.

37

The Little Toy Theatre

"That!" exclaimed Mr Penrose, pushing his chair away from the table and pulling out his napkin from under his chin, "was a perfectly splendid Christmas dinner."

His wife smiled. "Thank you, dear, but it's not over yet. There are tangerines and nuts to follow."

Mr Penrose groaned. "If so much as a segment of orange of a tiny walnut passed my lips I'd burst all my buttons on my new waistcoat." And he puffed himself to show everyone what might happen, which the children, George, Elizabeth and Anne, found most amusing.

Mrs Penrose rang for the maid to come and clear away, then the family made its way into the parlour. Mr Penrose promptly collapsed into his favourite armchair and the children set about playing with the presents they had opened that morning.

George emptied a box of shiny, red-uniformed, metal soldiers onto the floor and began setting them out. "Well you be the blue army, Father, so that I can have a battle?"

Mr Penrose had been planning to have a quiet snooze, but he cheerfully lowered himself onto his knees and lined up the blue-coated opposition.

Elizabeth had been given a toy sewing machine for Christmas and was planning to make her dolls a new wardrobe of clothes.

"You will help me, won't you?" she begged her mother.

On hearing this, little Anne quickly looked up. "But you promised you'd help me," she whined. "You know I can't do it on my own, it's much too hard." Her present was a toy theatre made of card, complete with scenery, actors and play to perform. Unfortunately for Anne, it all had to be cut out and stuck together before she could play with it.

"I know I said I'd help you," said her mother," and so I shall, as soon as I've cut out something for Elizabeth to sew. Now be a good girl and bring me my workbox."

Slowly the little theatre began to take shape. George left the battle he was fighting to fix the stage together. Elizabeth put aside the party frock she was making for her best doll to help her sister cut out the characters and stick them to long strips of card with which they could be moved about. When it was finished, Anne was eager to put on a show.

"I think you ought to practice first," suggested her mother.

"Of course," said Anne. "But you don't practice – you rehearse."

George and Elizabeth wanted to join in. "Which play shall we do?" they asked.

"Sleeping Beauty," said Anne.

George groaned. "Why, there are hardly any fights or battles in 'Sleeping Beauty'."

"Good!" chorused the sisters. Then the threesome huddled together behind the sofa to rehearse.

After tea, Mr and Mrs Penrose, cook and Sarah, the maid, were called into the parlour and shown where to sit. Elizabeth played a little tune on the piano then joined her brother and sister behind a table on which was set a toy theatre. The curtain was about to go up.

Apart from some scenery getting stuck and one or two of the actors falling over, the first part of the play went well. First there was the christening, where the wicked fairy puts a curse on the baby Princess, followed by the sixteenth birthday party, where the Princess pricks her finger and falls asleep for a hundred years.

It was where the prince meet a character called Ogre Frostytoes that things started to go wrong. George, who was doing their voices and moving them, thought that things needed livening up.

"Take that, you ugly ogre," said the Prince, jabbing the ogre with his sword.

"I'm not ugly," growled Ogre Frostytoes, jumping up and down on the Prince. None of it was in the script.

Anne was horrified. "Stop it," she cried. "Stop it at once. You're messing everything up. Oh, please tell him to stop, Father."

Mr Penrose was trying not to laugh. "Now that's enough, George. If you're not careful you'll do some damage."

But it was too late. The little toy theatre had already begun to come apart. George saw what was happening and stopped.

"I am sorry, Anne," he said. "I didn't mean to do that I can stick it together again. You'll see."

Anne wasn't listening. She had fled to the nursery in tears and she even though it was Christmas, that was where she stayed for the rest of the day.

When Anne opened her eyes the next morning the first thing she saw was the toy theatre sitting on the table at the end of her bed. George, who'd been waiting for her to wake up, popped his head round the door. "It's as good as new, Anne I promise you. Er, you're not still cross with me, are you?" he asked, anxiously.

Anne gave a weak smile and tried to shake her head, but it hurt. Her throat hurt too and her eyes felt hot. George called his parents who hurried to the nursery.

"She has a slight temperature," said Mrs Penrose, "but I don't think we need call for the doctor. We'll keep her in bed today and see how she is tomorrow."

"What about tonight?" whispered Mr Penrose. "What about the pantomime?" his wife shook her head and he gave a sigh. He had planned a surprise trip to see a real production of 'Sleeping Beauty' and he knew how disappointed she would be. She tried not to show it when her brother and sister popped in to say 'goodnight' before they left for the theatre, but when they had gone, she thought about them, dressed in their best clothes waiting for the thrilling moment when the curtain would rise and the play begin, and two tears trickled down her cheeks and plopped onto the eiderdown.

She dozed for a while and then something made her open her eyes and look at the little theatre. It seemed different, as though it was lit up and the Fairy Queen, who was standing in the centre of the stage, didn't look like a paper cut-out at all, she looked real. When she started to speak, Anne knew that she was real.

"Quite and still! Do not make a sound!
Wherever I am there is magic around.
A tale I will conjure of a King and a Queen,
Their daughter; a Princess, the loveliest ever seen.
Of good and of evil and a Prince, oh so bold!
So with no more ado, let our story unfold!

And unfold it did. Anne watched her little cut-out players perform 'Sleeping Beauty' for her eyes alone. And finally, when the Prince woke the Princess with a kiss, Anne drifted off into a deep, peaceful sleep.

The next day Anne was feeling much better.

"I didn't miss the pantomime after all," she told her family. "The little people in my toy theatre came alive and did 'Sleeping Beauty' just for me."

"That's funny," said Mr Penrose, "the people we saw in 'Sleeping Beauty' were just like the cardboard cut-outs."

George sniggered at his father's joke. "But it's true," Anne insisted. "When George put my theatre there yesterday, the Fairy Queen was alone on the stage, now there's the King and Queen and Sleeping Beauty and the Prince too."

"Perhaps you put them there and then forgot," suggested Elizabeth

"No, I don't," said Anne starting to get tearful.

Mrs Penrose intervened. "If Anne said it happened, then it happened. We'll let her get some rest and perhaps she'll be well enough to come downstairs for lunch. There's cold turkey, Christmas pudding and trifle – your favourite."

When everyone had gone, Anne clambered to the bottom of her bed and picked up some of her cut-out characters. They seemed so lifeless in her hand that she was beginning to think she had dreamt it all. Then she noticed something glinting in a corner of her theatre and she held between her fingers the tiniest of silver needles. It was much smaller than any in her mother's workbox and just like the one on which Sleeping Beauty pricked her finger in the play!

The Night Before Christmas

'Twas the night before Christmas,
when all through the house,
Not a creature was stirring,
not even a mouse;

The stockings were hung by the
chimney with care,
In hopes that St. Nicholas soon
would be there;

The children were nestled
all snug in their beds,
While visions of sugar-plums
danced in their heads;

And Mamma in her 'kerchief, and I in my cap,
Had just settled our brains for a long winter's nap;
When out on the lawn there arose such a clatter,
I sprang from the bed to see what was the matter.

Away to the window I flew like a flash,
Tore open the shutters, and threw up the sash.
The moon on the breast of the new-fallen snow,
Gave the lustre of midday to objects below;

When, what to my wondering eyes should appear,
But a miniature sleigh and eight tiny reindeer,
With a little old driver, so lively and quick,
I knew in a moment, it must be St. Nick.

More rapid than eagles his coursers they came,
And he whistled, and shouted, and called them by name;
"Now, Dasher! now, Dancer! now, Prancer and Vixen!
On, Comet! on, Cupid! on, Donder and Blitzen!

To the top of the porch! To the top of the wall!
Now dash away! Dash away! Dash away all!
As dry leaves that before the wild hurricane fly,
When they meet with an obstacle, mount to the sky,
So up to the house-top the coursers they flew,
With a sleigh full of toys, and St. Nicholas too.
And then in a twinkling, I heard on roof,
The prancing and pawing, of each little hoof.

As I drew in my head, and was turning around,
Down the chimney St. Nicholas came with a bound.
He was dressed all in fur, from his head to his foot,
And his clothes were all tarnished with ashes and soot;
A bundle of toys he had flung on his back,
And he looked like a pedlar just opening his pack.

His eyes – how they twinkled! His dimples how merry!
His cheeks were like roses, his nose like a cherry!
His droll little mouth was drawn like a bow,
And the beard on his chin was as white as the snow;
The stump of pipe he held tight in his teeth,
And the smoke it encircled his head
like a wreath;

He had a broad face and a little round belly,
That shook when he laughed, like a bowlful of jelly.
He was chubby and plump, a right jolly old elf,
And I laughed when I saw him, in spite of myself.
A wink in his eye and a twist of his head,
Soon gave me to know I had nothing to dread.

He spoke not a word, but went straight to his work,
And filled all the stockings; then turned with a jerk,
And laying his finger aside of his nose,
And giving a nod, up the chimney he rose;

He sprang to his sleigh, to his team gave a whistle,
And away they all flew like the down of a thistle.
But I heard him exclaim, ere he drove out of sight,
"Happy Christmas to all, and to all a good night!"

Santa's Best Coat

It was Christmas Eve and the Head gnome at the Gnometown Cleaners had just finished pressing Santa Claus's best red coat. "All those soot marks have come off," he said about the white fur round the collar. "Now it looks as good as new."

The Head gnome folded the coat carefully and put it in a large cardboard box. "Now take this along to Santa Claus right away," he told the smaller gnome.

So the smallest gnome set off, carrying the box carefully. He had quite a long way to go and the box seemed to get heavier and heavier with every step. "Oh dear," sighed the smallest gnome, as he walked through winter Wood. "I do wish I could have a rest for a few minutes."

Then he saw a large, hollow tree. "Just the place," he said to himself. "I will be sheltered from the wind in there."

So he squeezed through the hole into the tree. Then he put down the box and sat on a pile of dry leaves he found there.

The smallest gnome only meant to rest for a little while, but soon he felt very drowsy and fell fast asleep.

Much higher in the tree there lived Sammy Squirrel and he was curled up on his bed of dry leaves. Suddenly he began to shiver. "It's getting much colder," thought Sammy. "I really need some more bedding."

So he jumped out of bed and looked out of his front door. "Goodness, it's beginning to snow," he cried. "I had better go and get some more dry leaves."

Sammy scurried down the tree trunk and hopped through the hole at the bottom. There he saw the smallest gnome, fast asleep. "Someone else is using my spare bedding," sighed Sammy. "What shall I do?"

Then he saw the box which the smallest gnome had put on the ground. He lifted the lid and inside saw Santa's best red coat. "This will be much warmer than leaves," chuckled Sammy, and he slipped in between the folds of the coat and pulled the lid back over himself.

After a while the smallest gnome woke up. "Oh dear, it's getting dark," he gasped. "I shall have to hurry or Santa won't get his best red coat back in time to wear it tonight."

He looked out of the hollow tree and saw the snow, which was getting really deep. Then he saw something moving through the wood towards him. It was Rudolph, Santa's reindeer.

"Santa sent me to fetch his best red coat," said Rudolph. "He's been waiting for it all afternoon. Where have you been?"

"I feel asleep," confessed the smallest gnome.

"Dear me," said Rudolph, shaking his head. "You'd better ride on my back or Santa will be late starting to-night."

So the smallest gnome lifted the box onto Rudolph's back. It's heavier than ever," he puffed, not realising that Sammy Squirrel was still curled up inside.

Off they trotted, through the wood, until at last they saw the lights shining through the windows of Santa's house. Santa himself was waiting by the open door in his shirtsleeves.

"Have you cleaned my coat well?" he asked.

"Oh, yes," replied the smallest gnome, proudly putting the box on the table and opening the lid.

"Goodness me, whoever is this?" cried Santa. Sammy Squirrel lay curled up on the coat, still fast asleep.

"Wake up!" called Santa. "You can't stay here. We'll have to take you back to the wood."

So Santa put on his best coat, and Sammy and the smallest gnome climbed on the sleigh with him. First, Santa took Sammy Squirrel back to his tree house in Winter Wood and gave him a cosy quilt from a toy doll's bed to keep him warm.

"Oh, thank you," murmured Sammy, sleepily. "This will keep me warm for the rest of the winter."

Then Santa took the smallest gnome back to Gnometown and pulled a big parcel from the back of the sleigh.

"Perhaps this will help you to make your deliveries on time," he chuckled, as he drove away with Rudolph pulling his sleigh over the snow.

"Thank you," called the smallest gnome, waving until they were out of sight. Then he quickly pulled all the wrappings off the big parcel.

Inside was a shiny new bicycle with a big carrier basket on the front.

"It's just what I wanted!" cried the smallest gnome, jumping on and pedaling round and round with excitement.

"This will make my work much easier in future."

So now the smallest gnome could make his deliveries at top speed, and Santa never had any trouble getting his best red coat back in time from the cleaners again.

The Twelve Days of Christmas

On the first day of Christmas,
My true love sent to me:
A partridge in a pear tree.

On the second day of Christmas,
My true love sent to me:
Two turtle doves,
and
A partridge in a pear tree.

On the third day of Christmas,
My true love sent to me:
Three French hens,
Two turtle doves,
and
A partridge in a pear tree.

On the forth day of Christmas,
My true love sent to me:
Four colly birds,
Three French hens,
Two turtle doves,
and
A partridge in a pear tree.

On the fifth day of Christmas,
My true love sent to me:
Five gold rings,
Four colly birds,
Three French hens,
Two turtle doves,
and
A partridge in a pear tree.

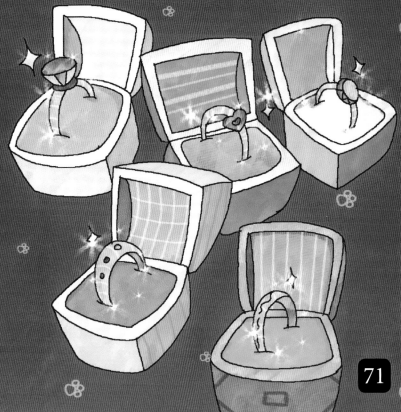

On the sixth day of Christmas,
My true love sent to me:
Six geese a-laying,
Five gold rings,
Four colly birds,
Three French hens,
Two turtle doves,
and
A partridge in a pear tree.

The seventh day of Christmas,
My true love sent to me:
Seven swans a-swimming,
Six geese a-laying,
Five gold rings,
Four colly birds,
Three French hens,
Two turtle doves,
and
A partridge in a pear tree.

On the eighth day of Christmas,
My true love sent to me:
Eight maids a-milking,
Seven swans a-swimming,
Six geese a-laying,
Five gold rings,
Four colly birds,
Three French hens,
Two turtle doves,
and
A partridge in a pear tree.

On the ninth day of Christmas,
My true love sent to me:
Nine drummers drumming,
Eight maids a-milking,
Seven swans a-swimming,
Six geese a-laying,
Five gold rings,
Four colly birds,
Three French hens,
Two turtle doves,
and
A partridge in a pear tree.

On the tenth day of Christmas,
My true love sent to me:
Ten pipers piping,
Nine drummers drumming,
Eight maids a-milking,
Seven swans a-swimming,
Six geese a-laying,
Five gold rings,
Four colly birds,
Three French hens,
Two turtle doves,
and
A partridge in a pear tree.

On the eleventh day of Christmas,
My true love sent to me:
Eleven ladies dancing,
Ten pipers piping,
Nine drummers drumming,
Eight maids a-milking,
Seven swans a-swimming,
Six geese a-laying,
Five gold rings,
Four colly birds,
Three French hens,
Two turtle doves,
and
A partridge in a pear tree.

On the twelfth day of Christmas,
My true love sent to me:
Twelve lords a-leaping,
Eleven ladies dancing,
Ten pipers piping,
Nine drummers drumming,
Eight maids a-milking,
Seven swans a-swimming,
Six geese a-laying,
Five gold rings,
Four colly birds,
Three French hens,
Two turtle doves,
and...
A partridge in a pear tree.

The King Who Cancelled Christmas

Long ago in far off country there lived a King who ruled fairly but not wisely and he often took days off. He never worked hard and didn't expect his subjects to either. His son loved him but thought he was a lazy King who spent too many days enjoying himself and throwing parties and trying to take days off.

"That pimple on my nose seems to have disappeared," he would say to his wife. "I think I'll declare a national holiday in its honour." And from then on that day would be known as 'Passing of the Pimple Day'.

There was also 'Toenail Trimming Tuesday', 'Dog Bathing Day' and 'Fish Paste Friday' which was a bit like 'Pancake Day'.

There were so many holidays that very little work got done. No crops grew, no houses were built and the children hardly ever went to school. The country got poorer, people went hungry and boys and girls grew up not knowing their alphabet.

When the King died, his son came to power and everything changed. He abolished most of the silly holidays introduced by his father, which at first, wasn't popular with his subjects for they had grown lazy and workshy. But when digging in the fields, sawing wood and hammering in nails, they followed the new King's example and began to work hard just like the new King.

Gradually the country grew rich again. But, although he could afford to take things easier, the new King worked harder than ever.

"Please turn down the lamps and let us go to sleep," begged the Queen. "It's way past midnight."

The King was sitting up in bed polishing his riding boots.

"And why are you cleaning those? You never go riding."

"No dear. Riding's a complete waste of time and energy. I've much more important things to do like weeding the flower beds and cutting the lawns." The King gazed around the room. "Would you like me to shine your dancing shoes while I'm at it?"

"What on earth for?" snapped the Queen. "I never go dancing. When was the last time we gave a ball or party? We don't even celebrate my birthday anymore," she said, sadly.

The King gave a grin. "Would you mind moving your head so I can polish those bed knobs?"

His wife let out a scream of exasperation and threw a pillow at him.

It was autumn and Queen was looking forward to Christmas. I She was discussing all the arrangements with the Chancellor when the King rushed in clutching a calendar. She was immediately filled with dread.

"I've thought how we can fit more working days into the year," he exclaimed, pleased with himself.

"What do we want with more working days?" asked the Queen, "haven't we enough already?"

"No, my dear, there are never enough. Why there's that order for eight hundred milking stools for the King of Lagunia and six hundred christening spoons for the....."

"All right, all right," said the Queen impatiently. "What are you getting rid of this time, 'Pudding Mixing Friday', 'Present Wrapping Wednesday' or 'Snowman Sunday'?"

"Christmas Day," he replied.

"Christmas Day!" echoed the Queen, horrified. "But you can't. I'm making plans."

"Exactly," said the King. "If I get rid of Christmas all those other days go too. They won't be necessary." He turned to the Chancellor. "Put out a decree at once that this year Christmas will be cancelled."

"Oh will it?" thought the Queen. "We'll see about that."

His subjects weren't very pleased with the news, but they simply grumbled amongst themselves and hoped the King would change his mind.

He didn't.

The night before Christmas Eve, the Queen lay awake waiting for her husband to fall asleep. Then, as soon as she heard midnight chime, she slipped out of bed and crept round the castle changing the date on all the calendars. Instead of reading December 24th, as it was now Christmas Eve, she had put them forward to the 25th - Christmas Day. Then she went back to bed to wait for morning.

"Would you believe it it's Christ... er, December 25th already?" said the King. "Doesn't time fly? Well I'd better be off. I've got to clear the snow off the castle drawbridge. There weren't any presents, I mean parcels left for me, were there?"

The Queen shook her head and the King left, looking disappointed.

It was lunchtime when they met again, seated either end of the long banqueting table.

"It does look gloomy in here," commented the King. "Don't you think a few decorations might brighten it up a bit?" he suggested.

"They might," said the Queen, "but with everyone working it hardly seems worth doing. Ah, lunch."

A servant placed before them plates of bread and cheese. The King's face fell. "No turkey? No stuffing? No cranberry sauce?"

"No dear," answered the Queen. "This an everyday working lunch."

The King spent a cold afternoon breaking the ice that had formed on the castle horse troughs. When he came in at tea time he was looking forward to a slice of iced fruit cake, but all he got was bread and dripping.

"I don't suppose there's a mince pie or two lying around?" he asked.

"Oh, no," the Queen told him. "I only make those at Christmas."

The King looked thoroughly miserable.

"I think I may have made a terrible mistake, cancelling Christmas," he sighed. "I miss the presents, the decorations, the food and we will have to wait a whole year to enjoy it next time."

The queen decided that he had learned his lesson and it was time to tell him about the trick she had played. "...and so you see, dear, it's still only Christmas Eve," she explained.

The King gave a whoop of joy and sent out messengers to tell all his subjects that tomorrow was a holiday and that they should stop work and prepare for Christmas Day.

And when the Queen's birthday came round again, he threw the biggest party that the castle had ever seen!

The Nativity Play

"Please, Miss! Joseph's supposed to come with me, not the three Wise Men," complained the Virgin Mary.

"Yes, Cathy, I know," said the teacher wearily. But you mustn't stop every time some little thing goes wrong. Haven't you heard the saying 'the show must go on'?"

From the blank look on Cathy's face it was evident that she hadn't.

"It means," Mrs Peel went on, "that whatever happens don't stop, keep going if the scenery falls down, or your costume falls down or the actor falls down. Now, let's start again, please try to get it right."

Mrs Peel nodded to the piano and for the umpteenth time that afternoon Mrs Graham played the opening bars to 'Once In Royal David's City'.

Inglenook Infants were rehearsing their nativity play. The school was famous for it. It was put on every year, all the parents came to see it and it usually went very well, but this year nothing seemed to be going right.

Mrs Peel had never done the nativity before. It had always been left to Mrs Morris to organize, but she had retired that summer and the Headmistress had asked Mrs Peel to take on the task. "I'm sure you'll make a wonderful job of it," the Head had said.

Mrs Peel had thought so too at the time, but now she wasn't so sure. Joseph couldn't remember where he was supposed to stand, the wise men kept fidgeting and the Shepherds giggled all the time.

The school bell rang out - it was going home time.

"Please, Miss. Can my auntie come and see the play as well as my mum and dad?" asked Pearl Wilson.

"I expect so," sighed Mrs Peel, although she couldn't imagine why Pearl's auntie or anyone would want to sit through this shambles of a Christmas story.

The next morning there was more rehearsing; this time in costume and on the stage in the big hall.

Someone's mum who kept horses had provided bales of straw to dot about the stage. Mr Green, the school caretaker, had built a stable and a manger and hung up a large star which, when it worked, lit up. It all looked marvellous and Mrs Peel hoped that once the children put on costumes and got amongst the scenery that it would all come right.

Once again the piano struck up with 'Once In Royal David's City...' and Joseph stepped on the hem of Mary's robe so she couldn't move.

"Please. Miss!"

"Keep going, Cathy, keep going," Mrs Peel urged.

This time everyone got onto the stage, but the Wise Men kept starting into the hall forgetting to sing and one of the Shepherds was making rude noises to make the others laugh.

"Sam Stevens, stop giggling," she called trying not to lose her patience. "And hold your lamb properly." They giggled all the more.

They hadn't even managed a complete run through when the dinner bell sounded. The performance was to be that afternoon.

Those in the play were allowed to stay in costume and eat a packed lunched up on the stage while the other infants had their dinners on the long tables down on the hall floor. It made the cast feel really important.

Alan, one of the Wise Men, started to show off while 'Miss' wasn't looking. He threw a piece of cheese and pickle sandwich at a Shepherd but it missed and fell into the manger, where it remained.

After lunch, the tables were cleared away and the benches were turned to face the stage. It wasn't long before parents started to arrive and take their seats for the show.

In a nearby classroom the cast waited for their cue to begin.

"Now, please, dears, sing your words clearly, try not to step on each other's clothes and don't gaze around the room," Mrs Peel told them. "It's the baby Jesus you should be looking at not someone's auntie in the front row." The children giggled, nervously.

"Good luck," she added, as the familiar strains of 'Once in Royal David's City' rang out.

Singing sweetly, they filed onto the stage. First Joseph and then Mary, who laid the baby Jesus in the manger.

As she did so she gave a small gasp and Mrs Peel, who was watching from the side of the stage, thought that something had gone wrong and that Cathy was going to stop. But, to her great relief, Cathy did as she'd been told and kept singing and staring wide-eyed into the manger.

As Joseph, the Wise Men and the Shepherds gathered round, they too could see what had made Cathy gasp. It was a little brown mouse sitting in the straw, nibbling a piece of cheese and pickle sandwich which Alan had thrown at lunchtime. It didn't seem the least bit worried about the singing or the presence of a large china doll.

With eyes glued to the munching mouse, the children sang their way through 'The Holly and The Ivy', 'The First Noel' and 'O Come All Ye faithful', to which everyone joined in.

Mrs Peel was delighted. They looked a picture grouped, around the manger gazing down at the baby Jesus. It was really quite moving. One or two of the mums were having to dab their eyes with handkerchiefs.

When it was all over the children dashed back on stage to look in the manger, but the mouse had gone.

"So that's why none of you could take your eyes off the manger," said Mrs Peel, after Cathy had told her about the mouse.

"It must have come out of one of those bales of straw, "said one of the boys, pointing. Mrs Peel shivered. "Well I hope it's gone back there." She wasn't too keen on mice.

The Headmistress tapped her on the shoulder. "Well done, Mrs Peel. A perfectly splendid nativity." Then she lowered her voice. "This year's infants can be a bit of a handful at times. But there they were today, standing round the manger looking just like little angels. I don't know how you did it!"

And Mrs Peel wasn't about to tell her that the success of that year's nativity was entirely due to a little brown mouse and a piece of cheese and pickle sandwich.